The Bobbsey Twins
on Blueberry Island

New edition! Revised and abridged

By Laura Lee Hope

Cover illustration by Pepe Gonzalez
Illustrated by Laurie Harden

Publishers · GROSSET & DUNLAP · New York

Look for these new
BOBBSEY TWINS® reissues:

Revised and abridged by Nancy S. Axelrad.

Contents

■ 1 ■

Mystery Bag

"Snap! Oh, Sna-ap!" called six-year-old Freddie Bobbsey. Anxiously he looked around the dock of his father's lumberyard on Lake Metoka. "Snap, where are you?"

"He's gone!" Flossie cried.

She was Freddie's twin sister and had blond hair and blue eyes like her brother.

Hearing the younger children's cries, Bert and Nan hurried toward them. They were twins, too. They were twelve and had dark hair and brown eyes.

"What's the matter?" Bert asked.

When Freddie and Flossie explained that the Bobbseys' dog, Snap, was missing, Nan said, "We'd better find him."

The twins glanced across the shimmering water at several green wooded islands that dotted the lake. Among them was Blueberry Island, where the Bobbsey family and Bert's

1

friend Charlie Mason were going camping for a week. They were leaving on Friday—only four days away. In preparation the older children and their parents had started cleaning the family's launch, the *Tall Timber*.

Now Freddie looked back at the lake's grassy shoreline. "There's Snap!" he shouted.

"Where?" Flossie asked.

"There!" exclaimed her brother, pointing to the white dog running between two rows of trees. "Snap has a bag in his mouth!"

Shouting the dog's name, the four children ran from the dock to the shore. Instantly Snap darted out of the shade and shot away.

"Stop him, Freddie!" Bert said as the animal sped past the boy.

Snap stopped, then lowered his front legs and growled playfully.

"What's in the bag, Snap?" Freddie asked. "Bring it to me."

The wary animal circled Freddie while the other children crept forward. In a sudden, quick move Bert grabbed Snap's collar.

"Somebody take the bag," he said, "while I hold him."

Flossie took the bag from Snap's mouth and opened it. Inside was a box with pictures of money on it.

"It's a game!" Flossie exclaimed, laying it on the ground.

Nan bent down next to her sister and helped her open the box. "It's a money game," she said. "See, these are fake coins and fake dollar bills."

"Ooh! We're rich!" Flossie giggled.

Nan began to flip through the bills. "There's a lot of real money mixed in with these phony bills!" she exclaimed. She held up a stack of ten-dollar bills bound with a purple band. The amount, $500, was stamped on it in large black numerals.

"Wow! Five hundred dollars in tens!" Bert cried. "May I look at it?"

As he took the money, Nan said, "Look. There's some handwriting on the band."

"It says, 'Aunt Emma's Money,'" Bert read aloud. Just then Mr. and Mrs. Bobbsey called the twins back to the launch. "Come on," Bert said. "Let's show Dad and Mom what Snap found!"

Bert stuffed everything into the bag and raced to the dock with the other twins. They reached it just as Charlie Mason rode up on his bicycle.

"How's it going, Bert?" he asked. "I came to see if there's anything I can do to help before we leave on our trip."

3

"Not a thing," Bert said, looking at the neatly swabbed deck of the *Tall Timber*. "But guess what Snap just found."

"What?" Charlie asked.

When the twins told their parents and Charlie about Snap's discovery, Mr. Bobbsey exclaimed, "That's amazing!"

"Who would hide money in a game?" asked Mrs. Bobbsey.

"It sure is mysterious," Charlie remarked.

After counting the real money, Bert announced there was only four hundred and ninety dollars in the pack. "Someone must have removed a ten-dollar bill."

At that moment Snap leapt forward and snatched the money from Bert's hand.

"No, Snap!" shouted Flossie as all the twins ran after the scampering pet.

Snap bounded just beyond their reach, and then dashed to the end of the dock.

"Stop him before he jumps—" Nan yelled.

But the dog had already plunged into the water.

"Oh!" cried Flossie. "The money will get lost!"

Bert kicked off his sneakers. Then he, too, dived into the lake.

"Snap can swim pretty fast," Nan said worriedly.

"Snap! Come back here!" Mr. Bobbsey commanded.

Obediently the dog turned and, swimming clear of Bert, disappeared beneath the dock.

"Oh! Here he comes!" Nan exclaimed.

Snap clambered up the bank and headed toward the children.

"The money's gone!" Freddie moaned.

Snap shook himself, showering the twins with water. Then Nan walked toward Bert, who was just climbing up the side of the dock.

"Snap lost the money, Bert!" Nan called. "It must be in the lake."

Bert dived in again and vanished under the dock. Soon he bobbed to the surface.

Above him stood Freddie, peering through a large crack between the boards. "I think I see the money, Bert," Freddie said. "There's something purple floating underneath here."

Bert swam under the dock.

"He's got it!" exclaimed Freddie.

Bert climbed onto the dock again, triumphantly holding the precious money.

"Good work, son!" Mr. Bobbsey said. He took the dripping bills and counted them. "The money is all here and in good condition."

"We'd better take it to the police station," Bert said.

"Right," his father replied. "But first we'll stop

at home so you can put on dry clothes. See you Friday, Charlie."

"Yes, sir! I can't wait to go to Blueberry Island!" Charlie said happily. "This is going to be a great summer vacation."

Charlie whistled as he rode away on his bike, and the twins climbed into the van with Mr. and Mrs. Bobbsey. Snap jumped to his usual place in the rear of the vehicle.

A short while later the family reached home. Bert hurried upstairs to change his clothes. Meanwhile, Freddie and Flossie ran to the kitchen with Snap. They found Dinah Johnson, the family's housekeeper, baking a cake.

She and her husband, Sam, who was the foreman at Mr. Bobbsey's lumberyard, lived in a cottage behind the house.

When the children told her about their latest discovery, Dinah exclaimed, "Don't tell me you found another mystery!"

Flossie nodded. "Yes, and we have to give the money back to Aunt Emma," she said.

"Snap found the money," Freddie explained to Dinah.

"That makes Snap a hero," said Dinah, going to the refrigerator. "I'll give him a nice big steak bone as a reward."

Snap sat on his haunches and cocked his head to one side. Snoop, the Bobbseys' black cat, meowed from a corner as if to say, "That lucky dog!"

Then Bert came into the kitchen. "Time to go," he said. The four children set off with Mr. Bobbsey for the police station.

Upon their arrival, Chief Mahoney greeted them with a pleasant smile. "Hello, everyone!"

Bert told how Snap had found the bag containing the mysterious money. "And this is the packet of real bills that was in the box with the play money," he said, handing it to the chief.

"I'll give you a receipt for this," the chief replied after he finished counting. "We've had no report of lost money lately. We'll hold it here long enough to give the owner plenty of time to make a claim. If no one does, the money will go to the finder."

"What will Snap do with all that money?" Flossie asked.

"Buy dog biscuits, I guess," Freddie joked.

The chief laughed. "I imagine he'll be glad to turn the money over to the Bobbsey twins."

"But we want Aunt Emma to have it," Nan said earnestly.

"I expect we'll hear from her," Chief Mahoney assured the twins. He gave a receipt to Bert. On it was written the amount of money that had been found and the date, June 24. "Here you are. Now hang on to it."

8

"Yes, Chief," Bert said. "And thanks."

The Bobbseys were about to leave the police station, when a woman burst in. She looked very upset.

"I've been robbed! All my money was stolen!" she exclaimed to the lieutenant at the desk.

The twins looked at one another. Was this Aunt Emma?

■ 2 ■

Bert's Puzzle

The Bobbseys waited eagerly to hear what else the woman had to say.

"Please start from the beginning," the lieutenant requested. "First, what is your name?"

"Anne Stevens."

She wasn't Aunt Emma! the twins thought, feeling disappointed.

"Someone grabbed my pocketbook as I was getting onto the bus to go home," the woman continued.

"That's the tenth report of a theft we've had in the last few days," the chief said, his mouth fixed in a thin line.

"I wish we could stay and help catch the thieves," Bert said, "but we're going camping for a week."

"You have fun," Chief Mahoney said. "If the thieves aren't in jail by the time you come home, I'll let you know."

"Okay!" Bert grinned. The children said good-bye to Chief Mahoney and stepped outside with their father.

"I think we ought to run an ad in the *Lakeport News* to tell Aunt Emma that we found her money," Bert suggested when they reached the van.

"If we write the ad today, we can phone it in to the newspaper right away," Nan said.

"That's a good idea," Bert agreed. "Now the only other thing I have to worry about is my project for the school fair this fall."

"What is it?" Nan asked excitedly.

"I want to make a labyrinth," Bert answered. "It's a little tricky to do, so I'm going to make a trial labyrinth first on Blueberry Island."

"If Mr. Harper agrees, that is," Mr. Bobbsey said, driving back to the Bobbseys' house. "He owns the property we'll be camping on."

"What's that big word, Bert?" Flossie asked, puzzled.

"Labyrinth," Bert repeated slowly. "It's a maze. It's sort of like the computer game we play at home, but much bigger. It will be thirty feet square—about half the size of the baseball diamond at Lakeport Elementary.

"The maze will be made of dirt paths and hedges," Bert went on. "The object is to get to the center and out again. It's not easy because many of the paths are dead ends."

Freddie's eyes opened wide with interest.

"If my trial labyrinth turns out okay, I'll build another one on the playground at school," Bert continued. "The only difference between the two will be that I'll use real bushes on the island and cardboard ones at school."

Bert went on to say that Mr. Tetlow, their principal, had approved the project for the school fair to be held in late September. Mr. Tetlow also said there could be an admission charge to enter the maze, since the fair was expected to raise money for new athletic equipment.

"A prize will be given to anyone who figures out the key," Bert concluded.

"What's the key?" asked Freddie.

"It's the secret of how to get to the center of the maze and out again," Bert replied. "The key is like a little road map."

Bert explained that in olden days in Europe, the gardens of kings were often made in the form of labyrinths. "The paths were so mixed up no one could find the center unless he knew the key.

"There are a lot of bushes growing wild on the island, so we'll be able to make a labyrinth like the old royal ones," Bert said.

"We'll all help you, Bert," Nan put in.

"Maybe Sam can help, too, if Mr. Harper

gives us the go-ahead," Mr. Bobbsey said. "I'll ask him."

"Great. Sam can cut through some of the bushes to make the paths," Bert remarked as they reached home.

While Mr. Bobbsey went to telephone Mr. Harper, the children gathered in the living room. Bert took a small notebook out of his pocket and began composing the advertisement for the *Lakeport News*.

After jotting several lines, he asked, "How's this? 'Found. Aunt Emma's money. Person must show proof of ownership. Write the Bobbsey twins, Lakeport.'"

"That sounds okay. The only thing I'd add is today's date, when the money was found," Nan suggested.

While Bert was writing down the information, his father emerged from the hallway.

"Good news, son! Mr. Harper says it's okay for you to build your labyrinth," Mr. Bobbsey announced. "I'll ask Sam to help us pack whatever tools you need and to come with us to the island."

"Hooray!" Bert exclaimed.

He showed the ad to his father and went to call the newspaper.

Afterward, he rejoined the other children. "The ad will be in tomorrow's paper," Bert said.

"Then there's a chance we could hear from Aunt Emma before we leave on Friday," Nan commented.

"I hope we do!" Flossie said.

"Me, too!" her twin chimed in.

The next three days passed quickly as the Bobbseys prepared for their trip. On the fourth day, Friday, Bert woke up early to help Sam put a load of camping equipment into the van. There were several new tents, sleeping bags, a grill, and numerous hampers of cooking utensils and supplies.

"There's enough gear here for a whole month!" Sam said with a laugh, sliding the last hamper across the backseat.

"We Bobbseys like to travel well prepared." Bert chuckled.

When they arrived at the lumberyard, Bert unloaded the fishing rods. "I hope we catch a big trout," he said.

"A bass or pickerel would be nice, too," Sam added.

They stowed their equipment on the launch. The last item to go aboard was a long, razor-sharp saw. "Your father told me you want to clear away the branches to make the paths," Sam remarked. "This will do the job beautifully. But promise me you won't try to use the saw yourself."

At that moment a noisy motorboat sped past the dock. Bert could see two people aboard, but he could not distinguish them clearly. Both wore red windbreakers with hoods that were pulled down low over their foreheads. As soon as the boat was fully out of sight, the sound of the motor stopped.

"That's odd," Sam said. "I wonder where that boat docked. I don't know of any landing place near here."

"Maybe it's tied up to a tree along the shore," Bert suggested.

"It's possible, I suppose," Sam said in a doubtful tone.

He pulled the van out of the lumberyard driveway and headed back to the Bobbseys' house with Bert. When they turned onto their street, Bert noticed the mail carrier walking briskly up the family's front walk.

"Any mail for us?" Bert called through the van window.

"Yes, quite a bit today," came the reply.

As soon as Sam had parked the van and shut off the engine, Bert got out and took the pile of letters from the mailbox. Near the top was an envelope addressed to: *The Bobbsey twins, Lakeport.*

"This must be an answer to our ad!" Bert said as he and Sam went inside.

Nan and the younger twins ran to greet them.

"We got a letter! You open it, Nan," said Bert. He handed it to her as cheers rang out from Freddie and Flossie.

Sam disappeared into the kitchen, and Nan went to the living room desk to get a letter opener. She carefully slit the envelope as the others waited to hear what was inside.

■ 3 ■
Steady Start

"Is the letter from Aunt Emma?" Flossie asked.

"Yes!" Nan replied. "And she lives on Blueberry Island!"

The twins hurried into the dining room, where Mr. and Mrs. Bobbsey were already seated. The morning newspaper lay partly open on the table.

"Nan, read the letter to us!" Freddie pleaded.

"Okay, here's what it says." Nan read aloud:

"The money you found is mine. My niece lost it on June 24. Bring the money to me because I hurt my leg and cannot get around. I live in a cabin on the north end of Blueberry Island.
                    Mrs. Emma Whiteside"

"Let's get the money from the police and take it to her," Flossie urged.

"First we need proof that she's the rightful owner," Bert said. "Mrs. Whiteside doesn't give any in her letter."

"That's right. She should be able to tell us where she got the money," Mr. Bobbsey said. "The pack of ten-dollar bills looked new—as if it just came from a bank. The owner should know which bank it is."

At this moment Dinah came in with a freshly baked coffee cake.

"While we're on the island and Dinah's here, who'll make all the blueberry pies and muffins?" Nan asked.

"Well, we can't bake at camp," her mother replied. "But if the blueberries are ripe, we can bring some home for Dinah to use in her baking."

"In the meantime, you'll have plenty of homemade cookies to take along," Dinah said. "When are you planning to leave, Mrs. Bobbsey?"

"As soon as we finish packing," she answered.

Mr. Bobbsey glanced at the front page of the morning newspaper. "Here's an article about the recent robberies in town," he said. "The police are warning everyone to be on guard. Besides the purse snatching and shoplifting, two houses have been burglarized, so doors and windows should be kept locked when no one is at home."

"We'd better tell Dinah to be very careful," Nan said. "Snap won't be here to bark at strangers."

"Maybe Snoop can meow extra loud," Freddie said.

"Do the police have any leads?" Bert asked.

"Someone reported seeing a red-haired man and a woman with curly blond hair running out of a store," his father replied. "But the police suspect there may be a whole gang of people involved."

As the children went upstairs to finish packing, Mrs. Bobbsey called to Bert, "We'll be leaving soon. Why don't you tell Charlie to bring his things over?"

"Sure, Mom," Bert answered. He went to the phone and dialed the Masons' number.

Shortly after Charlie arrived, the family loaded their bags into the van. Snap perched on a suitcase in the rear, and all the children piled in.

Freddie had a glum expression on his face.

"What's the matter?" Nan asked.

"I lost my flashlight in the backyard." Freddie pouted. "I wanted to take it to Blueberry Island."

Mr. Bobbsey overheard his son's remark.

"Don't worry about it. You'll find it when we get back. Anyway, Sam packed plenty of flashlights, including a big one if we need it."

When they pulled up to the boathouse at the lumberyard, Sam was there to meet them. After Bert and Charlie unloaded the rest of the baggage, Mr. Bobbsey drove the van into the garage nearby.

"All aboard!" called Sam from the launch.

Snap barked and followed the children to the boathouse. Inside was the *Tall Timber,* a thirty-foot open launch with a cabin forward for the captain and passengers. All the baggage was stowed near the stern, at the back of the boat. The camping equipment was put in a dinghy that was tied to the launch.

Sam took the wheel and guided the launch out onto the tranquil lake. Suddenly a small motorboat shot past them. The pilot, who was alone, wore a red windbreaker with a hood.

"Sam and I saw him early this morning. He sure whips up a lot of speed," said Bert.

"I like Sam's steady pace better," Mrs. Bobbsey said.

"I do, too," Freddie said.

Upon reaching deeper water, Freddie asked if they could see the other islands before going to Blueberry Island.

Mr. Bobbsey nodded, and the launch cruised

through the tree-lined channels. Bert looked around for the motorboat but did not see it.

"Dad, when we get to Blueberry Island, may we go see Mrs. Whiteside first?" Nan asked.

"Oh, yes!" Flossie urged.

"We might as well, before we unload," Mr. Bobbsey replied.

Now the *Tall Timber* headed for the north end of Blueberry Island. Mr. Bobbsey took out his binoculars. Looking through them, he said, "I see a dock up there."

Sam steered toward a ramshackle pier in a small inlet and docked the launch. Nearby on a cleared strip of land stood three small frame houses. Two of them were painted a drab gray and seemed to be vacant. The third was light yellow and had white-shuttered windows. A bicycle was on the porch.

"Does Mrs. Whiteside live there?" Flossie asked.

"We'll soon find out," her mother replied.

The group stepped out of the launch and went up to the cabin. Mrs. Bobbsey knocked, and the door was soon opened by an attractive-looking woman.

Two small children clung to her skirt. Mrs. Bobbsey introduced herself and the twins and said they were looking for Mrs. Whiteside.

"My name is Mrs. Turner—Emily Turner,"

the young woman said. "I don't know anyone named Whiteside. But there's a cabin on the other side of the woods. I think it has occupants now, although I haven't met them. Follow the path to your right and you'll find it."

Snap wagged his tail as the Turner children patted his head.

Nan noticed the bicycle and asked, "Do you have any other children, Mrs. Turner?"

The woman nodded. "I have a son who's ten," she said. "Ever since my husband died, Tommy has been a big help to me. You may see him if you go berry picking."

The Bobbseys thanked her for the information and told her they planned to camp on the south end of the island.

"Have a good time," the woman said. The campers left and proceeded through the woods of stunted oak and pine.

"Ooh, it's dark and spooky in here!" Flossie remarked.

The underbrush along the path was so thick that the group had to walk single file. Suddenly they heard branches crash beside them. A young fawn sprinted out of the woods, nearly bumping into Flossie.

"Oh! What a cute little deer!" she exclaimed.

The startled fawn took another leap and disappeared into the bushes.

Bert turned to Charlie, who was behind him. "Something must have frightened that animal to make it run out in front of us like that."

"I agree," Charlie said. "Every once in a while I hear the bushes crackle. It sounds like someone or something is following us."

As they walked on, both boys listened and watched for further evidence. They saw no one, but heard the same rustling of branches. Snap darted off the path twice, but since he did not bark, the boys were not alarmed.

Finally Mr. Bobbsey, who was in the lead, came to a clearing. "There's the cabin," he said as the rest of the group caught up.

Surrounded by pine trees, the building was no more than a tumbledown shack that sat near the water's edge. Next to it was a boathouse largely hidden by trees and shrubbery.

"Nobody's here," Freddie said. "There are boards over the windows."

"It does look deserted," Mr. Bobbsey agreed, "but I'll knock on the door anyway."

"Look at Snap!" Flossie said.

The shaggy white fur at the back of Snap's neck was standing on end, and he was growling softly. Sam clipped the leash onto the dog's collar.

"Snap doesn't like this place at all," Sam said.

Mr. Bobbsey stepped onto the rickety porch

and knocked on the door. There was no answer.

Bert was still convinced that someone was in the woods behind them. He quickly turned to look back. No one was in sight, but the leaves of a low tree were moving briskly. Since there wasn't any wind, someone must have shaken them!

Mr. Bobbsey knocked on the door again. This time a voice from inside the cabin answered, "Open the door and come in." The voice was cracked and hoarse.

Mr. Bobbsey lifted the iron latch and pushed the door open on its creaking hinges. The room beyond was dim.

Snap growled and Sam had to restrain him until the others had gone inside.

"Well!" said the hoarse voice sharply. "Did the whole town come?"

As their eyes grew accustomed to the dimness, the Bobbseys saw that the words had been spoken by an old woman in a wheelchair. She sat far back in a dark corner. A few pieces of old furniture were scattered about the room, and piled against the walls were suitcases. Clothing spilled out of them.

Mr. Bobbsey introduced himself and the others, but the woman did not give her name.

She narrowed her eyes at the children. "If you're the Bobbsey twins, where is my money?"

▪ 4 ▪
Strange Meeting

It was clear from what the woman said that she was Mrs. Whiteside.

Nan and the younger children stood next to Bert. "We're the Bobbsey twins," Bert said. "All of our family and Sam and my friend Charlie are camping out for a week on the other side of the island." Bert did not answer Mrs. Whiteside's question about the money.

"How nice," the woman said sarcastically.

All this time Flossie had been looking around the room. "Freddie," she whispered, "why does she keep it so dark?"

"Maybe her eyes hurt, or else she doesn't want us to see how messy her house is," Freddie replied.

Mrs. Whiteside could not hear what the younger twins were saying, because she was talking loudly. "That money is mine," she cried, "and I want it back!"

"How much money did you lose?" Bert asked calmly.

"Five hundred dollars," flared the woman. "The amount was marked on the purple band around it."

"There wasn't that much in the pack we found," Bert said. "Some had been taken out."

"What? Oh, that wicked girl!" snapped Mrs. Whiteside. "She stole some of my money."

"What girl?" Nan asked.

"My niece."

As Mrs. Whiteside spoke, Snap pricked up his ears. He turned his attention to the closed door that led to an adjacent room.

Charlie, who had observed the dog's behavior, also looked at the door. He heard a faint sound, as though someone were brushing against the door on the other side. No one else seemed aware of the noise.

Mr. Bobbsey concluded the visit by saying to the woman, "I'm afraid you'll have to show some proof that the money belongs to you."

"I told you how much was there before my niece stole some of it. I also told you about the purple band around the bills. What more do you want to know?" Mrs. Whiteside demanded.

"If you give us the name of your bank, we can check on the withdrawal," Mr. Bobbsey explained.

"Pshaw!" the woman said. "The money is mine, so give it to me now."

"There's another way to tell if it's your money," Freddie piped up. "Was it in a package with anything else?"

Ignoring the boy's question, Mrs. Whiteside gave her wheelchair an impatient shove. "Pen!" she shouted. "Pen! Come here!"

"Oh, look!" gasped Freddie, pointing.

The wheelchair had rammed against a long iron pipe that rested against the shadowy wall behind Mrs. Whiteside. The pipe slid across one of the boarded-up windows and fell with a bang.

From the rafters overhead came an eerie rattling and bumping noise. Then, as everyone stared up into the cobwebby darkness, a huge bat swooped down over Nan's head. She ducked quickly, and Flossie let out a piercing scream.

Mrs. Bobbsey put an arm around Flossie while Sam opened the door to the porch. The boys and Mr. Bobbsey drove the bat outside.

In the midst of the confusion, the closed door that Snap had been watching swung open, and a man stepped out. He had brown hair, and his clothes hung loosely over his large frame.

"Pen, son, make these people give me my money," Mrs. Whiteside said in a complaining voice.

Mr. Bobbsey spoke before the man could an-

swer. "You must realize, sir, that we'll need proof that your mother is the rightful owner before the money can be turned over to her."

"She doesn't need proof. You'd better give her that wad of bills if you know what's good for you," Pen threatened.

Mr. Bobbsey motioned for everyone to leave. "We'll be at the south end of the island this week. If you can produce evidence that the money is yours, I'll see to it that you get it. Good day, Mrs. Whiteside."

Her son, who seemed ready for a fight, reddened in the face. He looked at Mr. Bobbsey, Sam, the two strong boys, and the dog, and realized there were too many for him to tackle alone.

Instead Pen changed his tone and said pleasantly, "The money came from a bank out of town. I don't know that I can get any kind of proof."

"When you do, let me know," Mr. Bobbsey said, and he walked out of the cabin.

Pen Whiteside's only reply was to slam the front door.

"What a mean man!" Bert said, following Charlie along the path. "I saw a leaf and a dried twig caught in the cuff of his trousers. I'll bet he was the one we heard in the woods."

"He must have climbed in through a back

window after we went into the cabin," Charlie said.

"I wonder why Pen couldn't have come to Lakeport for the money," Nan remarked. "From what Mrs. Whiteside wrote in her letter, I thought she lived alone."

"I thought so, too," Mr. Bobbsey said. "There's something suspicious about all of this."

As the campers left the woods, Charlie said, "Bert, something awful just occurred to me. If Pen thinks your dad has the money with him, he might come to camp after dark and try to find it."

"If he does, he'll have to sneak past Snap," Bert said confidently. "Anyhow, the money isn't here, so Pen won't find it."

When the group was safely back on the launch, Sam steered along the shore toward the southern tip of Blueberry Island. The area was wild and beautiful, its high banks covered with dense shrubbery.

"Here we are!" Mr. Bobbsey said as they rounded a point of land.

The launch had reached a small harbor that led to a narrow strip of sand. Mr. Bobbsey dropped anchor about thirty feet from shore. Then he and the older boys rowed the dinghy to the beach and unloaded the camping equipment. When they were finished, Mr. Bobbsey rowed back to fetch the others and the baggage.

"Isn't this place beautiful!" Mrs. Bobbsey exclaimed, stepping onto the white sand.

Flossie sniffed the air. It smelled of sweet ferns and pine trees. "Um! It smells good, too," she said.

Walking inland on a wooded path, the campers saw a clearing.

"It looks like a short walk from here to our campsite," Mr. Bobbsey observed. "Let's go." Everyone took a bag and followed him.

When they reached the clearing, they discovered that it was very large. The group would set up camp at the southern end, and Bert would build his maze at the northern end. Surrounding the area were pine and oak trees.

At the northern end of the clearing stood an enormous oak tree. It rose from a tangle of shrubbery and underbrush.

"That tree looks like a lighthouse," Freddie said.

Bert was awestruck by its size. "It will make a wonderful center for my labyrinth," he said. "Come on, Charlie. Let's bring the rest of the equipment up from the beach and set up the tents."

In less than an hour everything was done. "This place is terrific!" exclaimed Charlie, looking at the little colony of five tents. "Who sleeps where?" He and Bert had decided earlier that they would sleep under the stars.

Mr. Bobbsey answered Charlie. "The girls have one of the larger tents. Mrs. Bobbsey and I have another. Sam and Freddie each have a small tent. The fifth and biggest tent is for supplies. There's an extra tent and sleeping bag, too."

Charlie grinned. "Snap should have a pup tent," he joked.

Bert looked beyond the tents toward the oak tree and said, "Wow! Look at all those blueberry bushes. They'll make great walls for the maze!"

He took a piece of paper from his pocket and spread it out for Nan and Charlie to see. "Here's my design."

The maze was square and had only one opening for both entry and exit. Within the maze were many L-shaped paths that twisted and turned around a small rectangle in the center. The rectangle had an opening on one side.

"Only one path leads right to the center. The rest are blind alleys. We'll mark the paths with stakes and cord—" Suddenly Bert was interrupted by a loud scream from the woods.

"That's Flossie!" cried Nan.

▪ 5 ▪

Maze Trouble

Nan, Bert, and Charlie dashed across the clearing until they came to a clump of trees where Flossie was standing.

"Freddie and I were playing hide-and-seek. Then I saw some boy watching me!" Flossie said. "He was in those bushes. His face was all blue. Maybe he was Danny Rugg, up to one of his tricks."

Danny was Nan and Bert's classmate, who was known to play a lot of mean tricks—especially on the Bobbseys.

Angered by the mention of Danny's name, Bert pushed through the bushes. On the other side he caught sight of a boy running away. Although the boy looked smaller than Danny, Bert could not be certain he wasn't the bully.

Rejoining the others, Bert said, "If that was Danny I saw, we're in for trouble."

"What would he be doing here?" Nan asked.

"Danny can get to the moon if he wants to," Freddie piped up as he crawled out from behind a big log.

"Freddie! Is that where you were hiding?" his twin squealed.

"I got stuck on a nail or something," Freddie replied. "Look, Nan, I ripped my pants." He showed a long, jagged tear.

"Oh, my goodness," Nan said. She went to see what had caused the tear. "Bert, this log is hollow and there's a broken nail sticking out of it."

"The log was hollowed out on purpose," Bert said. "Something may have been nailed inside and rotted away. All that's left is part of the nail. I wonder what was hanging on it."

"It's certainly a mystery," Nan said.

While Freddie and Flossie went back to camp to play, the older twins paused to look at the bushes surrounding the giant oak tree that Bert had chosen as the center of his labyrinth.

"The bushes on this side almost completely hide the lower part of the tree trunk," Nan said. "I'll check to see if there are as many on the other side."

Circling the tree, she shouted, "Bert! Charlie! Come look at this. There are no bushes here."

Bert and Charlie joined Nan. She was seated on a wide tree stump that stood close to the large oak. Facing her was a small clearing.

"No bushes," Bert said. "I wonder why."

"This stump looks freshly cut," Nan remarked. "Someone must have been here recently and cut down the second tree and all the brush on this side."

"Bert, in your design the center is surrounded by bushes. There's only a small opening on one side," Charlie pointed out. "So how can this oak tree be the center of the maze with half the bushes missing?"

"We'll dig up some shrubbery at the edge of the clearing and plant it here to fill in the gap," Bert said.

Charlie looked at the large empty space on the side of the tree and groaned. "We'd better get started immediately."

"Wait here, Nan, while Charlie and I get our supplies," said Bert.

The boys made their way back across the clearing. When they reached camp, they saw Sam crawling out of the supplies tent. He was holding a fishing rod.

"Have you seen my duffel bag?" Bert asked Sam. "It has a steel measuring tape and a ball of cord in it. I need them to start laying out the maze."

"Your bag's in there"—Sam pointed to the tent—"with a bunch of wooden stakes I just made. Sorry I can't do more for you now. I'll help tomorrow. I'm going to catch some fish for our supper."

"I hope you get a whopper," Bert said. "I'm starting to get hungry!"

He dragged out the duffel bag and found the measuring tape and cord. Charlie picked up the bundle of stakes.

When the boys returned to the oak tree, they found Nan waiting for them. "I have something to show you," she said.

She led them to the north edge of the clearing. There she pointed to an opening in the bushes just large enough for one person to walk through.

"Won't this make a good entrance to the maze?" Nan asked.

"It will, if it's the right distance to the oak tree," Bert declared. "Let's measure." He took the steel tape from his pocket and handed one end to Charlie. "Please hold this and walk toward the oak."

"Sure," said Charlie, stepping forward. When he reached the tree, he stopped. "The tape measures fifteen feet exactly."

"Okay, good," Bert said.

"Now what do we do?" Nan asked.

"Let's mark off a thirty-foot square with the stakes and cord," her twin answered. "Then we'll lay out the paths the same way."

When this was done, Mr. and Mrs. Bobbsey came with the younger twins to see how the project was progressing. They observed the carefully placed stakes and cord-marked paths. "Looks like you've made a good start," Mr. Bobbsey said.

At that moment the aroma of grilled fish drifted across the clearing, and the group headed back.

"Supper's almost ready!" Sam announced.

While the older children went down to the lake to wash up, Mr. Bobbsey put corn on the grill to cook. Freddie and Flossie set out plates and napkins.

The campers ate heartily in the fresh, balmy air. They could hear the swaying trees rustle and the water lap gently against the shore.

Bert took second helpings of everything. "This bass is scrumptious," he said.

"Glad you like it," Sam answered, taking a piece of corn. "Everything tastes extra good in the fresh air."

"This supper is yummy!" Flossie chimed in.

When the meal was finished, the children played a game of catch. The younger twins tired quickly, however, and Mr. Bobbsey said, "It's time for bed, Freddie and Flossie. Pleasant dreams."

"'Night, Daddy," Flossie said, yawning.

A while later, as Bert and Charlie spread their sleeping bags out under the starry sky, Snap trotted toward them. He curled up happily between the boys and nuzzled Bert.

"You old rascal," Bert said, patting the dog's shaggy white head.

Bert gazed up at the sky, but only briefly. When he saw that Charlie was fast asleep, Bert shut his eyes, too.

He slept soundly until he was awakened by a thud in the distance. Someone or something had fallen. Snap rose instantly. Ears pointed up alert, he looked toward the woods, then bounded away into the darkness.

Bert did not move. He watched the dog leap out of sight, then return.

"Is everything all right, Snap?" Bert asked. Snap wagged his tail and lay down.

Soon he and the boy were sound asleep again.

As the first rays of sunlight broke through at dawn, Bert quickly got up and put on his sneakers. He remembered the unexplained noise he had heard during the night.

"Come on, Snap!" he said, heading across the clearing.

With the animal at his heels, Bert hurried to the big oak tree.

What he saw there made him gasp, "Oh, no!"

■ 6 ■
Hairy Clue

The cord that had been used to lay out the paths of the maze was piled in a tangled heap. Almost all of the stakes had disappeared!

"Nan! Charlie!" shouted Bert, running back to camp. "Someone wrecked the maze!"

"What?" Charlie said, astounded.

He zipped open his sleeping bag as the others came out of their tents.

"What did you say, Bert?" Nan asked groggily.

"The cord is down and almost all of the stakes are gone!" Bert explained. "I heard a noise last night that sounded like a thud. It woke me up. Snap ran into the woods to see where it came from."

"Where is Snap now?" Mr. Bobbsey asked.

"He must have stayed behind by the oak tree. He went there with me just a few minutes ago."

"Why would anyone want to spoil the labo—labo— the maze?" Freddie spoke up.

"I'll bet it was that mean Danny Rugg," declared Flossie, "trying to scare us again."

"Good thing we have enough cord to fix the paths this morning," Charlie said.

"What if they get messed up again tonight?" Bert asked anxiously.

"Snap and I will sleep over there to be sure they don't," Sam said. "I'll use the extra sleeping bag we brought. In the meantime, I want to do some inspecting with Snap."

He went off while the children helped Mrs. Bobbsey prepare breakfast. Soon the griddle began sizzling with golden pancakes.

As everyone ate, Bert said, "Dad, do you think Pen Whiteside took those stakes?"

"No, Bert. I think Mr. Whiteside is only interested in getting his hands on the money you found," Mr. Bobbsey answered.

"Whoever ruined the maze must want us to stop what we're doing an awful lot," Nan said. "If it's Danny, he's just being mean as usual."

"And what if it isn't Danny? What if it's someone else?" Bert asked.

Nan paused to think. "If it's someone else, I guess he just doesn't want us around," she said finally.

As Bert looked sadly toward the maze, Snap bounded into view. He was carrying something in his mouth and shaking it playfully.

"Oh! It's a bird!" Flossie cried.

"Snap doesn't catch birds," Bert reminded his sister. "He must have something else."

The dog dodged around the children, then stopped and let go of the mysterious object.

"Yuck. What is that?" Nan asked.

Bert gingerly held up a false hairpiece.

"Snap found our first clue!" Bert said. "Whoever was here last night lost a toupee."

"Wowee!" exclaimed Freddie.

"The owner is probably an older man," Mr. Bobbsey concluded.

"So he's not Danny Rugg," Charlie put in.

"Why do men wear wigs, Daddy?" Flossie asked.

"They wear toupees to cover up baldness," Mr. Bobbsey explained. "Did anyone notice if Pen Whiteside had one on?"

"I couldn't see him too clearly in that dark cabin, but I think his hair was the same shade of mousy brown as the toupee," Nan said.

"I guess Snap scared the guy away before he had time to hunt for it," Bert said.

"And before he could steal *all* the stakes," Nan added.

"Sam will have to cut more of them before we

can lay out those paths again," Charlie said.

Bert agreed. "I'm ready," he announced.

When the meal was over, Mr. Bobbsey said to Bert, "I'm glad you're not discouraged, son. While you and Charlie work on the maze with Sam, I'll take this toupee to the Lakeport police. I'll also bring back more cord."

"May I go with you, Dad?" Nan asked.

"Us too!" Freddie and Flossie chimed in.

"You three may go with me." Mr. Bobbsey smiled.

Mrs. Bobbsey said she would stay at camp.

In a little while the *Tall Timber* was skimming across Lake Metoka. As it approached the dock at the lumberyard, a motorboat zoomed past, cutting through the water at full speed.

"That's the same boat we saw yesterday," Freddie said.

"It made the waves slap hard against the *Tall Timber*," Flossie said.

Nan squinted her eyes in the sunlight to see who was aboard. There was only one person, the pilot. He was wearing the same red windbreaker he had worn the day before. His face was completely hidden from view.

Who is he? Nan wondered.

The launch was now back in the boathouse. Mr. Bobbsey and the children went to the garage, where the van was parked.

"Today's a big shopping day in town," Mr. Bobbsey said as the children climbed inside. "There are sales everywhere, so it'll be crowded. I'll try to park near the police station so we can scoot right back to the lumberyard."

As it happened, Mr. Bobbsey found a parking space only a block from the station. Nan took the hands of the younger children and followed her father to the station.

When they arrived, Nan told Chief Mahoney about the wrecked maze.

"Our dog found this in the same vicinity," Mr. Bobbsey said. He put the toupee on the chief's desk.

Chief Mahoney examined it. Then he said, "You'll be interested to know that no one has claimed that four hundred and ninety dollars."

"We put an ad about it in the newspaper," Nan told him.

"I saw it," the chief said. "Has anybody answered it yet?"

"Yes. A woman who lives on Blueberry Island," Nan replied. "We went to see her, and we asked her to give us proof that the money belongs to her."

"Well, if you get proof, I'll be more than happy to return the cash to her," the chief said.

As the group left the station, Mr. Bobbsey said, "There seems to be an awful lot of excitement in Lakeport these days—the kind we don't like. I hope it quiets down soon."

"It will when the thieves are caught," Nan declared.

When they reached the lumberyard again, the twins' father told the children to wait for him by the boathouse.

"I want to get some extra cord in my office for Bert. I won't be long," Mr. Bobbsey said.

A few minutes later, Freddie heard a swishing noise coming from the boathouse.

"What's that?" he asked, running toward the side door.

It sprang open, and a man wearing a cap darted out, nearly knocking Freddie into the water.

"Get out of the way," he muttered in a deep voice.

Before any of the children could stop him, he quickly turned the corner of the boathouse and disappeared behind a pile of lumber.

"I couldn't see his face too well," Freddie told his sisters, "but I know he had a mustache and his hair was red."

"We'd better tell Dad about him," Nan said.

When the children reached Mr. Bobbsey's office and told him about the man, he said, "We'll have to keep the boathouse locked from now on."

Mr. Bobbsey advised one of the workmen, then started for the boathouse.

"Daddy," said Freddie, coming to a halt, "the police said one of the thieves has red hair."

"But they didn't say he has a mustache," Mr. Bobbsey pointed out.

"You mean the man in the boathouse isn't the thief?" Freddie asked.

"No. I suppose the thief could have grown a mustache to disguise himself. But it's probably a coincidence that the two men have red hair," Mr. Bobbsey remarked, patting Freddie's shoulder. "Come on, let's go."

After boarding the *Tall Timber* once again, the Bobbseys headed across the glittering lake. When they reached Blueberry Island, Mr. Bobbsey gave Nan the cord to take to Bert. The children hurried to tell Bert and Charlie about their trip to Lakeport.

When they arrived, they found the boys and Sam hard at work on the maze. Sam had whittled a new bundle of stakes and untangled part of the cord, while the two friends were struggling to fix the rest.

"Hi!" Nan said, greeting the trio cheerfully. "This is from Dad."

Charlie was relieved to see the new ball of cord in her hands. "Am I glad you brought that," he said. "This is some mess."

Quickly Freddie told about his discovery of the man in the boathouse.

Sam and the boys listened with concern.

"Things are sure getting more mysterious," Sam said. "I don't like it a bit."

"It's creepy, if you ask me," Charlie agreed.

Nan tactfully changed the subject. "I'm here to help. What can I do, guys?"

"As soon as I clear the old cord out of the way, you can help me measure the paths again," Bert replied.

The children said no more about the recent events. They worked all afternoon until the sun vanished behind some passing clouds.

By evening the sky had cleared. "It's a super night," Bert said. "Would you mind, Dad, if Charlie and I slept on the deck of the *Tall Timber*?"

"Of course not," Mr. Bobbsey said. "Take your sleeping bags. Sam can row you out in the dinghy. Sound the horn when you want to come back in the morning."

"We will," Bert said. The boys went to get their bags and followed Sam to the small boat.

The lake looked like black crystal as Sam rowed through the darkness. Soon they reached the launch and the boys climbed aboard.

"Remember," Sam said, "if you want anything during the night, just blow that horn."

"Okay," Bert replied. "Good night, Sam."

"Sleep well, boys." With that, Sam pushed the dinghy's oars back through the water. Bert and Charlie crawled into their sleeping bags.

They lay back under the star-filled sky and talked about the mysterious intruder who had wrecked the maze. The rocking of the boat made them drowsy, however, and they stopped talking.

Bert was almost asleep when he heard something scrape softly against the side of the boat. He listened intently.

"There's a boat alongside," Bert whispered to Charlie. "I can hear the oars."

Then Charlie heard them, too. The sound was unmistakable. Oars were being dragged into a boat.

The boys got out of their sleeping bags and peered over the rail at a small rowboat. A man was tying it to the stern rail of the *Tall Timber*.

"Dad, is that you?" Bert called out.

There was no answer.

■ 7 ■

The Blue-Faced Boy

The stranger ducked his head and broke the cord, setting the rowboat free. He muttered something about a "mistake" as he pushed the oars back into the water. In a flash he was gone, lost in the darkness.

"That's odd," Charlie said.

"I wonder who he is," Bert said, "and what he wanted. Did you see his face?"

"No."

"Neither did I," Bert said. "I think he saw the *Tall Timber* in this inlet and figured there might be something worth stealing on board."

"Well, I wouldn't worry about it," Charlie answered. "I think we really scared the guy. He won't be back tonight."

"I agree. There's no point waking up the others."

Bert felt uneasy but soon managed to fall asleep. When the boys arose the next morning,

Bert scrambled to his feet and went to the stern rail. "Charlie! Look at this piece of cord! It might be a clue."

"What do you mean?" Charlie asked.

"It's some of the cord from the maze!" Bert exclaimed. "Maybe the guy who was here last night is the one who wrecked the labyrinth!"

Charlie stared wide-eyed as Bert glanced at his watch. "Hey, it's time for breakfast," Bert said. "Let's swim ashore and not bother Sam to come get us."

"I'll race you to the beach!" Charlie said with a laugh.

"You're on!"

The boys were wearing cotton shorts and T-shirts. They removed the shirts and tossed them into their sleeping bags, then dived into the water. The boys swam briskly toward the narrow strip of sand, where they saw Sam approaching from the wooded path.

He smiled at the boys when they reached shore.

"We thought we'd save you the trip," Bert said. "Did anyone show up at the labyrinth last night?"

"I didn't see anyone," Sam replied. "But Snap—he growled once and went sniffing around. Then he came back and lay down again. He was quiet the rest of the time. The maze looks fine today."

Relieved by the news, Bert and Charlie told about the stranger who had rowed to the launch during the night.

"If you're planning to spend tonight on the boat, I'll go with you," Sam said. "I'll take along my big flashlight and shine it in the fellow's face if he returns."

The boys changed into dry clothes, and then related the incident to the rest of the family.

When Mr. Bobbsey heard about the piece of cord that Bert had discovered tied to the stern rail, he said, "Bert, you're probably right about the man who visited the *Tall Timber* last night. No doubt he wrecked the maze, too."

"But why?" Nan asked.

No one, not even her father, had an answer.

"Well, we won't let any of this spoil our camping trip or the maze," concluded Mr. Bobbsey, winking at the twins' mother. "Mary, if you and I do the fishing today, Sam can devote his time to the maze."

"Fantastic!" Bert said. "Who's ready to work?"

There was a chorus of "We are!" and the children crossed the clearing to the oak tree. Sam trailed after them with his cutting tools.

"Bert, you tell us what to do," Nan said.

"All right," her brother replied. "Charlie and I will stake out the paths on the north side, and Nan, you run the cord along them. We'll help Sam dig up small bushes to use as a hedge between the paths."

"You're the boss," Sam said.

"Freddie and Flossie, you take away all the leaves and dried twigs, okay?" Bert directed.

"Right!" the younger twins said.

Work started at once. Bert went off to look over the proposed entrance to the maze.

No one had noticed his departure until a loud thump accompanied by a cry of "Ouch!" brought everyone to a halt. They turned to see Bert flat on the ground.

"Bert!" Nan shouted, running to his side.

Dizzily the boy sat up. He gaped at a cord stretched taut between the bushes at each side of the entrance.

"I tripped over that cord. It wasn't here yesterday," he said, wincing. "I twisted my ankle." As he rubbed it, he noticed something shiny in the grass. "What's this?"

"What's what?" Nan asked as her brother picked up a sparkling object.

"It's a diamond ring!" Nan exclaimed.

"Where did it come from?" Charlie asked.

"I don't know," Bert replied. "But I'll hang on to it until we can turn it over to the police.

Maybe it belongs to the man who lost his toupee."

"Or someone who was with him," Nan put in.

Sam and Charlie helped Bert to a grassy knoll on the bank of the lake. The bank rose high above the water and was covered with tall, thick weeds and dense shrubbery.

"You sit here and rest your foot," Sam told Bert.

"I'll stay with you," Flossie said, flopping down next to her brother.

She listened to the swish of the water below and soon got up to peer through the over-growth.

"Don't lean on those bushes!" Bert warned as he watched Flossie's body press forward. "Look out!"

The bushes parted, and Flossie plunged head-first! Bert dived after her. He grabbed her ankles and slid forward.

"Help!" Bert shouted.

Sam and Charlie came running. They pulled the two children back to safety.

"I almost fell into a boat down there," Flossie whimpered.

Bert pushed the curls out of her eyes. "What boat?" he asked.

"There was a boat with a man in it right under here," his sister replied.

Charlie rushed to the edge and pushed aside the bushes. "I don't see any boat," he said, scanning the lakeshore in both directions.

"It must have been a motorboat if it got away that fast!" Flossie said. "Look again, Charlie."

Nan, who had joined the group, also looked. "Maybe it was a log," she remarked.

"It wasn't," Flossie objected. "It was a boat with a man in it. I couldn't see his face very well, but he was wearing a cap and he looked awfully big."

"The man is gone," Bert said to appease Flossie. "We can't do anything about him now."

"We'd better get on with our work," Sam said. "Bert, you stay off that ankle of yours. Sit on this knoll till we're through."

Reluctantly the boy agreed, and the rest of the group returned to the maze.

It wasn't long before the children heard their parents' voices.

"Mommy and Daddy are back!" Freddie cried. "Let's go see if they caught some fish!" He and Flossie hurried away.

Nan, meanwhile, went to sit beside her brother.

"Now that I think about it," Bert said, "the water below here did sound as if it were lapping against something solid, like a boat."

"But how did the boat disappear so quickly?" Nan asked.

"I suppose it could have gone into a small cove."

When Freddie and Flossie told their parents about Bert's accident, Mr. and Mrs. Bobbsey hurried across the clearing to the knoll.

"How's your ankle, Bert?" his father asked.

"Not bad. It's just a slight sprain," the boy said. He explained how he had fallen, and showed the ring he had discovered on the ground.

"This looks like a very good diamond," Mrs. Bobbsey said. "Maybe a picnicker lost it."

"Or maybe the person who rigged the cord did, Mom," Bert suggested.

Nan saw the worried look in Mrs. Bobbsey's eyes. "Maybe you're right, and maybe Mom's right," she said. "Did you catch any fish, Dad?"

"You bet we did," Mr. Bobbsey said proudly. "A whole bucketful. I'm going to cook it for us."

"Then Charlie and I will go on measuring," Nan said.

As the grown-ups went back to camp, Bert hobbled over to the maze to watch the children. Presently a slight movement in the underbrush at the edge of the woods caught his attention. The bushes crackled, and out popped the head of a boy. There were blue smudges on his cheeks.

The boy with the blue face! Bert thought excitedly. "Hi!" he called.

The mysterious boy stepped in front of the startled children. He was almost as tall as Bert and had dark brown hair and eyes.

"My name is Tommy Turner," he said shyly, wiping a smudge of blue off his lips.

"Do you live on the north end of the island?" Bert asked.

"Yes. How did you know that?" Tommy answered in surprise.

"We met your family when we arrived," Bert said.

"I didn't mean to spy on you," Tommy continued. "I was only trying to figure out what you all were doing over there by the tree."

Just then, Freddie and Flossie came over to the maze.

"The blue-faced boy!" Flossie gasped.

"You're not Danny Rugg!" her twin said.

Nan introduced the children.

"Have you been eating blueberries?" asked Flossie.

Tommy nodded. "That's why my face looks blue," he said. "I pick lots of blueberries for my mom. She bakes pies and sells them to a store on Rand Island. It's a large island just north of here. A man is coming to get the pies tomorrow."

"Freddie and I can help you pick blueberries after lunch," Flossie offered. "Can you stay and eat with us?"

"That'd be great!" Tommy grinned.

"Would you like to see our labyrinth first?" Charlie asked. Tommy's eyes shifted to the stakes and transplanted hedges.

"Your what?" Tommy asked.

"It's a maze," explained Freddie. "It's like a puzzle, only it's a garden."

"It sure looks like a puzzle," Tommy said as he followed one of the paths. "I could really get mixed up in this."

Bert told him about the school fair and why he was making the maze. "Maybe you can come to the fair," Bert said.

Tommy smiled. "I'd like to." Then he followed the other children out of the maze.

Remembering that he had left his bucket behind the bushes, he went to fetch it.

When Tommy did not return, Charlie said, "I wonder what's keeping him."

Charlie stepped behind the tall shrubbery and called Tommy's name. A short distance away he heard twigs break underfoot, and Tommy answer, "My blueberry pail has disappeared!"

■ 8 ■

Hidden Loot

"Are you sure your pail is gone, Tommy?" Charlie asked.

"Yes, I looked everywhere," the boy said worriedly. "It had a lot of berries in it."

When Nan and Bert heard about the missing bucket, they joined the search but were no more successful than Tommy.

"We'll loan you a pail to use until you find your own," Nan said, leading the way to the campsite.

Mr. and Mrs. Bobbsey gave Tommy a warm welcome. In a little while the children were enjoying a picnic of sandwiches and cold drinks on the beach.

"Are there many paths in these woods?" Bert asked Tommy.

"Only three," Tommy answered. "One is the trail we took from your camp to the beach. Another runs from my house to a cabin."

"Where does the third one go?" Flossie asked.

"It goes from the cabin I mentioned through the woods to the big oak tree."

"Do you mean the oak tree in our maze?" asked Freddie.

"Yes," Tommy replied. He swallowed his last mouthful and got up to stretch. "Thanks a lot. That was a great lunch. I'd better go now and finish berry picking."

"Wait for us!" Freddie exclaimed. Flossie went to get two baskets.

"There are plenty of blueberries beyond the clearing," Tommy told the children. They trekked toward the underbrush. "Sometimes I wish I was an octopus with eight arms and a hand at the end of each one. Then I could pick a whole lot of blueberries all at once!"

Flossie and Freddie held out their hands. "We have four and you have two. That makes six hands!" Freddie exclaimed.

By day's end, several quarts of blueberries had been collected and one side of the maze was completely finished.

The children were pleased but also very tired. It wasn't long after supper that Bert and Charlie said they were ready to go to bed. Mr. Bobbsey offered to row them to the launch with Sam.

"I hope that man in the rowboat doesn't show

up again," Mr. Bobbsey said when he was ready to leave.

"We'll be on the lookout just in case," Bert said. "See you in the morning, Dad."

Sam had brought a flashlight along, ready to be turned on at the first sign of trouble. The three kept vigil for the mysterious caller until midnight. Then, unable to stay awake any longer, they settled down to sleep.

It was sometime later that Bert heard the splashing of oars nearby and roused Charlie.

"Wake up," Bert whispered.

Sam's eyes fluttered open, too. He quickly reached for the flashlight.

Quietly they all crept to the rail and looked below. A rowboat had pulled near the launch. Quickly Sam pressed the button of the flashlight, and a great beam of light arced over the boat.

For a fraction of a second the man stared up in confusion. He had red hair and a mustache.

"Who—" Bert started to ask.

But the stranger lowered his face, and with a mighty pull on the oars sent his boat toward the shore.

"Hey, stop!" Sam shouted. He pointed the flashlight out over the water trying to catch the man in its glow.

"The man Freddie saw in the boathouse had

61

red hair and a mustache," Bert said. "I wonder if there's a connection."

"Whoever he is, he's awfully strong," Charlie said. "He broke that heavy cord last night with one jerk."

The boys continued to wonder about the mysterious stranger. Bert said, "We'd better sleep in shifts in case he tries to sneak on board again."

It was decided that each of them would stand watch for two hours. Sam took the first shift. He settled himself in the stern with the flashlight as the two boys crawled into their sleeping bags.

Later, Sam awakened Charlie to take over. "No problems so far," Sam reported.

The rest of the night passed uneventfully. In the morning the boys told the others what had happened. Freddie and Flossie gasped when they heard that the night visitor looked like the man in the boathouse.

"Maybe he wants to steal the *Tall Timber*," Nan said.

"I hope not!" Flossie exclaimed.

"We all hope not," her mother said. "Now eat your breakfast. Tonight we'll build a bonfire and have a marshmallow roast. Okay?"

Flossie clapped her hands. "I love marshmallows!" she said.

After breakfast Mr. Bobbsey said he was taking the launch over to Rand Island. "I'm going to the little store there for some supplies."

"That's where Mrs. Turner's blueberry pies are sold," Freddie said. "May we go with you, Daddy?"

"Of course you may. I'll let you know when I'm ready to leave."

Freddie and Flossie caught up with the older children and Sam, who were headed to the maze. When they reached the oak tree, they broke into pleased grins. The north end with its tall, stately hedges and paths was completely finished.

"Now we can tackle the south end," Bert announced.

Sam gazed at the thicket. "I gather it's going to have plenty of L-shaped paths like the north end," he said.

"That's right," Bert said, grinning.

Sam smiled. "Where do you want me to start cutting?"

"I'll show you," Bert replied. "First I'll stretch the cord over the top of the bushes to mark where the paths should be. Then you cut between them."

Bert took a step back to begin and winced, feeling a sudden sharp pain in his ankle.

"You'd better sit down, Bert, before you make your ankle worse," Nan suggested. "Charlie and

I can lay out the cord for the paths."

Mr. Bobbsey, who had come to get Flossie and Freddie, overheard the remark. "Why don't you come with us, Bert?" he said. "You can rest your ankle on the boat."

"I think I will, Dad." Bert got to his feet and limped after his father and the twins.

Seated aboard the launch, Bert felt much better. He enjoyed the breeze blowing over the lake as they sped toward Rand Island.

Presently Flossie asked, "Are there any games on the *Tall Timber* that Freddie and I can play with, Daddy?"

Mr. Bobbsey, who was sitting at the wheel, glanced around the cabin. "If there are, they'd be in a locker, Floss," he said.

Together Flossie and Freddie lifted the lid of one of the heavy seat-lockers in the cabin. They stood still for a moment, staring at what was inside.

"Daddy!" Freddie cried. "There's a sack in here. Is it yours?"

"It's full of lumps!" Flossie said.

Bert hobbled toward the children as Freddie pulled out a small brown cloth bag.

"That's odd. I've never seen it before. I wonder where it came from," Mr. Bobbsey said. He watched Bert untie the rope that held the top of the sack together.

"Zowie!" exclaimed Freddie. "This bag is full of money and watches and jewelry."

"It's probably stolen property," said Mr. Bobbsey.

"Now we know what that red-haired guy was after last night," Bert declared. "He must have hidden all of this stuff here and was coming back for it."

"If he's the man I saw coming out of the boathouse," Freddie said, "I'll bet he hid everything in the *Tall Timber* before he came out."

"We'll take these things to the Lakeport police at once," Mr. Bobbsey said. He made a wide circle with the launch, passing Rand Island, and headed for the lumberyard dock.

Bert, meanwhile, took an empty duffel bag out of the locker and put the sack in it.

When they reached police headquarters, the chief smiled at them from behind his desk.

"No report on Aunt Emma's money yet," he said. "Nor on that toupee."

"We found more, Chief," Bert declared. He handed over the diamond ring, and his father produced the duffel bag.

Chief Mahoney gave a long whistle as he took the articles out of the bag and laid them on his desk. There were watches, bracelets, rings, wallets, loose change, and numerous rolls of bills.

"Where did you find this stuff?" he asked.

"On our boat," Freddie said. Then Bert told about the man who had tried to come aboard two nights in a row.

"This is a very important discovery," the chief said to the Bobbseys. "I'm going to call some of the people who have been robbed and see if these things belong to them. Then they can claim their possessions, thanks to you."

As they left the police station, Mr. Bobbsey said they would do a few errands in town, then return to the lumberyard.

"Before we go, I want to investigate the boathouse and see if the man left any other clues behind," Bert said.

They returned to the lumberyard within the hour, and Mr. Bobbsey unlocked the boathouse. After searching inside and out for clues, the children finally gave up. At that moment they heard a noisy motorboat sputtering along the lakeshore.

It was the same boat that had whizzed by twice before. Again it seemed to slip out of sight and then stop.

"I'd like to know where that boat goes," Bert said as he followed his father into the boathouse with Freddie and Flossie.

"There's an old loading wharf at the edge of the lumberyard," Mr. Bobbsey said. "It was used years ago when the lumber company loaded large vessels directly from the tramway."

"What's a tramway?" Freddie asked.

"It's a track that wagons run on," his father said.

"Like a railroad track?" asked Freddie.

"Yes. But the old wharf is pretty high for passengers in a small boat to step onto," Mr. Bobbsey explained. "They'd have to have long legs."

"Let's take a look at it anyway," Bert said as his father steered the launch along the shore.

"There's the old wharf," Mr. Bobbsey said. "It's almost hidden by trees now."

The group peered at the darkened wharf but could see nothing at first. Then Freddie opened the locker and took out a pair of binoculars. He held them to his eyes.

"Oh! I see something!" Freddie exclaimed.

■ 9 ■

Vanishing Suspects

"What do you see?" Bert asked.

"The motorboat and a chain ladder. The ladder is hanging down from the wharf right over the boat!" Freddie replied. "But I don't see anybody." He handed the binoculars to Bert. "You look."

Bert stared ahead as the launch came to a halt. "Yes, that's the same boat. Freddie's right. But nobody is in it."

"Maybe the man is hiding on the floor," said Flossie. "It's spooky here. Let's go!"

As her father swung the launch in a wide circle, he said, "The next time I go into town I'll tell the police about this fellow and his free parking place."

Back on Blueberry Island, Flossie reported everything with great enthusiasm.

"So the loot is what our visitor wanted!" exclaimed Charlie.

"If he shows up again tonight," Bert said confidently, "I'll tell him he can find his stuff at the police station."

During the afternoon the children worked with Sam on the maze. "All it needs is a little sprucing up," Sam said, "and it'll be a real beauty."

"I just love working on the maze, but I wouldn't want to get lost in it," Flossie said.

That night the family gathered on the beach for supper. A gentle wind blew whiffs of pine scent as the children roasted marshmallows for dessert.

"These are the best," Nan said, tasting a marshmallow that was toasted a light golden-brown.

"I wish I could cook them faster," Freddie said.

"Put two on a stick at one time," Nan suggested.

When all the marshmallows had been eaten, the children curled up on blankets and watched the twinkling lights of Lakeport across the water.

It was after ten o'clock when Sam and the older boys headed for the launch. Once again they took turns keeping watch.

Back at camp all was quiet until Snap sensed someone outside the girls' tent. He sat up with a start and bolted away, yapping at the unknown intruder.

Mr. Bobbsey ran from his tent and called to the dog, as did Nan and her mother, but this time Snap did not obey. There was no sound except the rustling of underbrush in the distance.

"Where is he?" Nan asked anxiously.

"He's probably chasing an animal," Mr. Bobbsey said. "He'll be back."

In the morning, when the boys and Sam came in from the launch, they found the whole family out whistling and calling Snap's name.

"What happened?" asked Bert.

"Snap chased someone away last night. He went so far he didn't come back," Freddie said unhappily.

Nan told about the camp visitor and how Snap had gone after him.

"I guess the man in the rowboat went ashore instead of coming to see us, Charlie," Bert concluded.

Sam, who had gone across the clearing to look for Snap, came hurrying back to the camp.

"Somebody wrecked the maze!" he burst out. "I didn't go through all of it, but the bushes at the entrance are down."

"Not again!" Charlie said in disgust.

"Snap must have chased the intruder into the

maze," Bert said. "No one would go in there purposely if he were trying to escape."

The children set to work repairing the maze. Nan asked the younger twins to gather the broken branches from the paths.

Freddie agreed and went to get some baskets that lay next to a tree. But when he saw something moving behind the thicket, he stopped.

If that's Tommy Turner, Freddie thought, *maybe he'll know where Snap is.*

To the boy's surprise, a young woman with long black hair appeared. She was wearing a bright yellow print skirt and a short-sleeved white blouse. Around her neck hung strings of brilliant red beads.

"I wonder where she came from," Nan murmured to the boys.

The woman walked quickly to the entrance of the maze. "What are you making here?" she asked. "I've never seen anything like it on Blueberry Island."

"Do you live here?" Nan inquired.

"No, I do not," the visitor said, tossing back her long, silky hair. "I come to pick berries every summer."

After Bert told about his school project, she asked, "Would you mind taking me through the maze? I'd like to see it."

"Not at all," Bert said. He led the woman along the twisting paths while Nan and the other children sat on the knoll.

Upon reaching the oak tree, the stranger turned abruptly and fingered her beads. Suddenly they flew in all directions. "Oh, I've broken my necklace!"

Bert stooped to pick up the beads.

"Don't bother," she said, clutching several she had caught in her hand. "They're not worth the trouble. Besides, I must go now. I don't have time to see the rest of the maze. Take me back the way we came in."

"Of course," Bert said. He led the way back to the entrance.

The visitor said no more to Bert, but paused to talk to the others. "Why do you all look so sad?" she asked.

"Our dog, Snap, ran away," Freddie said glumly.

"Is he white and sort of shaggy?"

The children nodded.

"I saw a dog like that tied to a tree deep in the woods when I came through today."

"That must be Snap!" Flossie exclaimed.

"Would you like me to take you there?" the woman asked.

"Oh, yes!" the children said.

The black-haired woman led the way into the woods. Though Bert tried to follow, his ankle throbbed, forcing him to turn back.

On the ground lay several red beads that the woman had apparently dropped. Bert put the beads in his pocket and went on.

At the labyrinth, he halted, stunned. Over the top of the hedge near the entrance he could see the head of an animal moving.

It's a big brown bear! Bert thought. *He's probably heading for camp. I've got to warn the others!*

Despite his injury, Bert hurried as fast as he could. Mrs. Bobbsey, who had heard Bert approaching, came out of the supplies tent.

"A bear is chasing me!" Bert yelled, and waved her back. He turned to look for the animal, but it was nowhere in sight.

"Where's Dad?" the boy said, panting.

"He's fishing with Sam—" began Mrs. Bobbsey. She quickly followed her son to the beach.

When they saw Bert waving frantically, the men rowed to shore.

"What's going on?" Mr. Bobbsey asked.

Bert explained, and the three grown-ups sped across the clearing to the maze. Seconds after Bert reached it, they all were astounded to see the back of a man's head rise over the top of a bush. He was bald.

"Did you see a bear?" Bert asked the man.

The bald head ducked out of sight.

Bert circled through the maze and back again. "He could've escaped through the entrance or the hedges and run into the woods," Bert concluded.

But when the Bobbseys explored the labyrinth, they found no broken bushes.

"He must have been hiding in a blind alley," Mr. Bobbsey said. "He probably waited for us to pass, then ran out."

Bert noticed a trail of red beads along the path from the oak tree to the entrance. "The woman we met today was marking the way for someone!"

They went into the woods to find the other children.

Meanwhile, Freddie and Flossie along with Nan and Charlie had followed the mysterious woman deep into the woods.

"Go in there between those two crooked trees," she said. "Walk straight ahead and you'll see your dog."

Charlie stepped toward the trees. But something made Nan hesitate.

The woman seized the girl's arm. "Go on!"

"Don't you push my sister!" Freddie said.

"I said go on." The stranger glared at the boy.

Nan took Freddie and Flossie by the hand. "Come on, we'll see if Snap is here," she said.

They caught up to Charlie, who was on the other side of the trees. "How much farther is it?" he asked.

He stared past Nan and gulped. She and the twins turned to see what was the matter.

The rude woman had vanished!

■ 10 ■

Double Discovery

"What a strange lady," Nan said. "She just left us here in the woods."

Immediately the children began circling the area, calling and whistling for Snap. The dog still did not answer.

"That woman is a meanie," Flossie said as the group started back to camp.

They had walked a short distance when they caught sight of Tommy. As he came toward them, Nan happened to glance at her arm.

"Oh! My bracelet's gone!" she cried.

"Did you lose it?" Charlie asked.

"No, I couldn't have. That awful woman must have slipped it off when she grabbed my arm."

When she and Charlie told Tommy about their latest encounter, Tommy said, "I saw a black-haired woman in a yellow print skirt and a white blouse go into the Whitesides' cabin this morning."

"That's interesting," Nan said.

"I wish I could help you look for her," Tommy said. "But I've got more berry picking to do before I go home."

The twins and Charlie waved good-bye to Tommy. On the way back to camp they met up with Bert and the grown-ups.

"I see you didn't find Snap," Bert greeted them, sounding disappointed.

"No, I'm sorry to say," Charlie replied. He told Bert about the mysterious woman. Nan explained that Tommy had seen the same woman enter the Whitesides' cabin.

"We'd better pay a visit to Mrs. Whiteside," declared Mr. Bobbsey, "right after lunch."

"I was hoping we could," Nan said.

She wondered what they would find in the old cabin at the north end of the island.

The cabin proved to be as desolate-looking as ever with the windows still boarded up. Mr. Bobbsey knocked several times before the cracked, hoarse voice asked them to come in.

Mrs. Whiteside was seated in her wheelchair in the same dark corner.

"It's about time you brought my money," she snapped.

"We didn't bring the money, Mrs. Whiteside," Nan said, stepping forward. "We came to ask if your niece has come back. We heard that a young—"

"Nobody has been here today," bristled Mrs. Whiteside. "Now what about my money?"

"We'll see that you get it as soon as we have proof of your ownership," Mr. Bobbsey said.

He opened the door and the visitors filed out. As they retreated onto the porch, Bert tripped on a loose board. Something in the crack caught his eye. It was a red bead!

He picked it up and put it in his pocket. When everyone was back on the launch, he held the bead next to the ones he had found in the maze. They matched!

"Another clue?" Charlie asked.

Bert nodded. "This proves that the woman we met was at Mrs. Whiteside's cabin. It also proves that she's connected to the man who was in the maze today."

Bert told about the bald-headed man. Not wishing to alarm the younger children, he did not mention the bear. "I found some red beads that were scattered by the woman. She must have been marking a trail for the man I saw."

"I want to see this trail of beads," Charlie said.

"I do, too, Bert," Nan said.

When the launch dropped anchor in the small harbor, Mr. Bobbsey rowed the older children to shore first. He warned them to be careful.

On the way to the maze Bert told about the bear he'd seen. "That's why we have to be extra careful," he said. "It's a mystery how the bear got in and out of the maze."

As he spoke, the bushes at the edge of the woods rustled noisily, and Tommy appeared. "Come quick!" he shouted.

"What's up?" Bert asked. The children ran to meet Tommy.

"I saw my berry bucket. It's on the porch of the Whitesides' cabin. I didn't dare get it, because a man was sitting there."

"Are you sure it's your bucket?" Charlie questioned.

"Yes. There's a streak of green paint on one side."

"Did the man you saw have mousy-brown hair?" Nan asked, thinking he was Pen Whiteside.

"No," Tommy answered. "He had red hair."

The children were excited by the news.

"The man must be a friend of Pen's," Bert said.

Was he the stranger who had hidden the sack of loot on the *Tall Timber*? Mrs. Whiteside, her son Pen, the black-haired woman, and the red-haired man all seemed to know each other. Two of them were thieves. Were the others dishonest, too?

That night Bert and his father stayed aboard the *Tall Timber* to guard it. Charlie remained at camp while Sam kept watch over the maze.

In the morning Flossie said, "Nobody came. Not even Snap." A tear trickled down her cheek.

"Don't cry, Floss," Bert said. "I'm going to climb to the top of the oak tree and look over the whole island for Snap. He can't be too far away."

While Bert went to borrow his father's binoculars, Nan comforted her sister. "Snap will come back. You'll see," she said.

Nan and Charlie followed Bert to the big oak tree. Bert slung the strap of the binoculars around his neck and climbed the trunk. From near the top he reported, "There's no sign of Snap. But I see the Whitesides' cabin. There's a motorboat tied up at their dock."

"I want to see it," Nan said. She climbed onto the broad stump by the tree. But as she jumped to reach the lowest branch, she thought she felt the stump shift under her feet. She decided it could be her imagination playing tricks. In a few minutes Nan reached the high branches, and Bert passed her the binoculars.

Through a gap in the leaves Nan could see the north end of the island including the Whitesides' cabin. She focused on the cabin as a young woman stepped into view. She wore a large, floppy straw hat that hid her face.

Nan watched the figure go to the boat, where a man in a red windbreaker sat waiting. "I'm sure that boat is the one we saw in Lakeport," Nan remarked.

Bert agreed.

By now Charlie had joined the twins. "There it goes! He's heading straight for Lakeport," he exclaimed.

At that moment, Flossie and Freddie arrived with Tommy.

"What do you see?" Flossie called up the tree.

The children climbed down and described the mysterious couple in the boat.

"Last night," Tommy said, "I saw that same motorboat. It always passes by our cabin when it goes to the boathouse near the Whitesides'."

"Is that where the boat is kept?" Bert asked.

"Oh, yes. It goes out almost every morning, and it comes back in the evening—sometimes not till late."

"Go on, Tommy," Nan said.

"When I went to bed, I saw the motorboat through my window. A little while later something woke me up. I looked out, and there in the moonlight, near shore, was a rowboat. I couldn't see the face of the man in it, but he had on a red windbreaker just like the one the man in the motorboat wears."

"Was he alone?" asked Charlie.

"Yes," Tommy replied, "but he must have had a heavy load, because the rowboat was low in the water and he wasn't going very fast. He was being real quiet."

"I want to find out more about those two," Bert said.

A little while later Sam joined the group. "Sam, we've got to go back to the Whitesides'," said Bert.

"Your mother and father went fishing," Sam said. "But I guess I can go over there with you."

"We can take the path near the entrance to the maze," Tommy said. "It goes right to the Whitesides' cabin. Follow me."

They walked along the path until they reached the tree-lined shore where the old cabin and boathouse stood. Tommy noticed that his bucket was no longer on the porch.

Bert and Charlie went ahead to look in the boathouse. "There's no boat here now," Bert announced when the boys returned. "But I saw oil on the water, so a motorboat must have been moored inside recently."

They went to the cabin and Sam knocked on the door. There was no answer. He tried opening it, but it wouldn't budge.

"Well, we can't break the door down," Bert said sullenly.

"What if Mrs. Whiteside is ill and needs help?" Nan said. "Can't you get the door open, Sam? Please try."

Bert pulled out his penknife and handed it to Sam. "This might do it," Sam said, inserting one of the blades between the frame and the door.

Suddenly they heard a click, and the old, warped door squeaked open.

Bert entered the cabin first, with the others close behind him. In the dim interior they could see the empty wheelchair in a corner.

"Mrs. Whiteside, are you here?" Nan called out. "If you need—"

Before another word was spoken, Flossie let out a frightened shriek. The others looked in her direction. They saw the head of a bear!

"It's not real, Flossie," Nan said as Bert went over to examine the shaggy brown head lying on a low chest by the door.

"Here's the rest of the costume," Charlie said. He pointed to a furry heap on a chair.

"That's the only kind of bear there could be on Blueberry Island," Tommy said with a laugh. "A make-believe one."

"I'll bet this is what I saw in the maze!" Bert exclaimed. He told Freddie and Flossie about the bear head peeking over the bushes.

"Pen Whiteside, or somebody else who lives here, must like to dress up," observed Nan. "Here's a box of wigs and toupees of all colors. There's a red mustache, too."

"The mustache is like the one the man in the boathouse had!" Freddie cried excitedly.

"It's also like the one the visitor to the *Tall Timber* had," Bert said.

"Mr. Pen Whiteside must have lots of different kinds of hair," Flossie said. "Snap found a toupee in the maze."

"If he's the one I saw in the maze yesterday," said Bert, "he's pretty bald."

"He probably didn't wear a wig then because he was using the bear head," Sam spoke up.

Flossie, meantime, had noticed a dress and shawl lying on the wheelchair. "Those are Mrs. Whiteside's clothes," she said.

"She probably wears a gray wig," commented Charlie, taking one out of a box.

"Maybe she's in the other room," Freddie suggested.

Bert knocked on the door. When there was no answer, he turned the knob and opened it.

For a while Bert said nothing.

"What's in there?" Nan asked.

Still too dumbstruck to answer, Bert gazed at the room beyond.

■ 11 ■

The Stump's Secret

"Wait till you see this!" Bert finally said as the children hovered next to him.

On the other side of the door was a small bedroom with a bed and a table. A cracked mirror hung over the table. Clothing spilled out from boxes and suitcases, which lay strewn across the floor. Other clothing hung on nails that had been driven into the bare walls. Nan and Flossie darted over to them.

"Here's a yellow print skirt and a white blouse!" Nan cried.

"And here are two wigs—a curly blond one and a long black one," Charlie said, lifting the half-opened cover of a box.

"The curly blond wig fits the description of the thief running out of the store," Nan said.

"And the black wig is what the woman with the red beads was wearing!" Bert added.

"So the black-haired woman, the blond

woman, and old Mrs. Whiteside must all be the same person using disguises!" exclaimed Nan.

"And I'll bet the man uses disguises, too," added Bert. "Like a red wig."

The Bobbsey twins looked at one another in astonishment. *They had solved the mystery of the Lakeport thieves!*

"We must tell the police!" Nan said.

"I wonder where the rest of the stolen loot is," said her twin brother, walking around the room.

"The bad man hid some of it on our boat," Flossie reminded Bert.

"I'm sure that's only a small part of the loot," Charlie said, "like the diamond ring Bert found."

"I don't think the five hundred dollars belongs to Mrs. Whiteside," Freddie said.

Nan heaved a sigh. "I wonder if we'll ever find the real owner."

"Even though these folks appear to be the thieves, we have no business snooping around like this," Sam said. "We'd better go."

The young detectives reluctantly left the cabin, and Tommy dashed around to the back. When he returned, he said, "I found my bucket!"

"Leave it for now, Tommy," Bert spoke up. "If you take it, the Whitesides will know that someone has been here. They might skip out before the police come. Did you find anything else?"

"Just a bunch of brown cloth bags and a couple of battered pans on a small grill."

"How big were the bags?" Bert asked.

"Not too big, and they were tied with rope."

"That's the kind of sack we found on the launch!" Bert exclaimed.

The children hurried through the woods and soon reached the maze. Nan suddenly halted as a thought came to her. She recalled the feeling she'd had when she jumped from the stump to a branch of the oak tree.

"There's something funny about that stump," Nan said. "This morning I thought it moved."

"It moved?" Sam repeated in bewilderment.

"Yes, let's take a closer look at it."

She ran through the entrance of the maze ahead of the others and followed the twisted path to the oak tree. The stump that stood beside the tree looked the same—broad, solid, and firmly rooted among low-growing weeds.

"Let's try to push it," Bert said.

"I'll do it," Sam said.

He squatted next to the stump and gave it a mighty shove. To everyone's surprise, the stump was so light that Sam toppled over with it in his arms!

"It's hollow!" Charlie cried.

"Look!" Flossie exclaimed. She pointed to a hole where the stump had been.

"There are steps going down into the ground!" Freddie said.

Sam got to his feet, and they all stared at the opening. It was large enough for a grown-up to climb through. Wooden planks were lined around it, and a small flight of crude steps reached down into a damp cave.

Bert let out a whistle. "It's a secret passage! This must be how the bald-headed man disappeared."

Sam, who had been examining the overturned stump, said, "There's a cleat nailed inside this."

"The man must have put it there so he could pull the stump back over the hole after he went down the steps," Bert said.

"That's sort of like the nail that was in the log that tore my pants," Freddie said.

"That log must have been the first cover the man used. When it rotted, he made this one," Bert said.

Bert and Sam went down the steps, followed by Charlie and the others. At the bottom they found a cave that extended under the labyrinth to the lake.

"I never dreamed there was such a place on the island!" Tommy said.

"Look, there's a pond," Nan said. She pointed

to where a glimmer of light shone dimly on the murky water.

"It must be an inlet from the lake that runs into the cave," Bert said. "There's so much shrubbery around the opening that it can't be seen from the outside."

Charlie craned his neck to look at the far end of the cave. "I see an empty rowboat tied up next to some bushes," he said.

"That's the boat I saw when I leaned over the bank and Bert caught me!" Flossie exclaimed.

"This is just about where the knoll is," Bert said, running forward. "No wonder the boat disappeared so fast—"

He was suddenly interrupted by a harsh rattling sound. All the children froze. The sound came from the darkest part of the cave.

Freddie darted ahead. "It's Snap!" he shouted.

The dog was whirling from side to side on the damp cave floor, trying to break loose from a heavy chain that hung from a thick collar. The chain was attached to a small post.

"Poor Snap! Why doesn't he bark?" Nan said, hurrying after Freddie with the others. As they drew closer, she saw the muzzle and bent to remove it.

"Snap, we missed you!" Freddie and Flossie exclaimed, putting their arms around the dog.

Snap whined with joy. He gave a few short barks and leapt to the foot of the steps.

"He wants us to leave," Sam said, "and so do I."

"Come on, everybody," Bert said. "We've got Snap, and we know how the man in the maze disappeared."

"We also found where the man in the rowboat hid," Flossie added.

Nan was the last to start up the crude stairway. As she did, she noticed a dark heap against the wall behind the steps.

"Oh, my goodness!" she gasped, going toward a pile of bulging brown cloth bags. Bert, Charlie, and Tommy hurried back down the steps after her.

Nan lifted one of the bags. "This is heavy," she said.

"Those bags look like the empty ones I saw behind the Whitesides' cabin," Tommy said excitedly. "What's in them?"

Bert untied one of the ropes and Nan peered inside. On top was a shining gold bracelet.

"My lost bracelet!" Nan exclaimed. She took it and slid it on her arm. "This loot probably belongs to that terrible woman who stole my bracelet."

"Her partner must be the man we saw in the motorboat," Bert concluded.

"I'm glad they're not here today," Charlie said. "But why did they steal Snap and tie him up?"

"They probably figured Snap would lead us to the stump's secret," Nan said.

From the top of the steps came several more barks.

"Snap wants you to come up here," Sam called. "What's keeping you?"

"Bert, hurry and tie up that bag," Tommy said.

Bert fastened the rope securely. Then he and the two boys followed Nan up the steps.

"We found more loot!" Charlie announced as Sam replaced the stump. Nan showed him her gold bracelet and told what the children had concluded about the thieves.

"Wonderful," Sam said, impressed. "Now no more dillydallying. We don't know when the thieves will return."

As they raced across the clearing, Tommy said, "I'll bet the Whitesides used their motorboat to bring all the stuff they stole in Lakeport to their boathouse on the island. Then Pen took it to the cave at night in the rowboat."

"But the rowboat was tied there at the cave," Charlie said, confused.

"He must have come on foot to get it. He used

the path from his cabin to the maze," Bert said. "Now I understand why the black-haired woman left the trail of red beads only from the oak tree to the entrance on the north side. It's the direction her partner would be coming from—the north end of the island, where the Whitesides' cabin is."

Out on the launch Mr. and Mrs. Bobbsey had heard Snap barking. They rowed ashore and hurried up the beach to meet Sam and the children.

"Mommy, Daddy!" yelled Flossie. "The stump isn't a stump at all, and Snap was chained up under it!"

"We found a pond under the ground with a boat in it!" Freddie said. The older children supplied the details.

When the children finished explaining, Mr. Bobbsey said, "We must report this to the police at once."

"I'd better stay here and guard the camp," Sam said.

"I'll wait with you," said Mrs. Bobbsey.

"And I'll go keep an eye on the Whitesides' cabin," Tommy said.

"Okay, but be careful," Mr. Bobbsey warned. He and the other children boarded the *Tall Timber* to head back to Lakeport.

"That woman is clever at disguises," Nan said. "I wonder what her real name is. I doubt that it's Whiteside."

"She probably has a police record," Bert said.

Before he could say another word, a noisy motorboat shot across the lake. It carried two people—a woman holding a large, floppy straw hat, and a man in a red windbreaker and hood.

"There they are again!" Bert exclaimed.

▪ 12 ▪
Trapped!

For a moment it looked as though the speeding boat would collide with the launch, but Mr. Bobbsey swerved out of the way.

"Whew!" exclaimed Bert as the thieves' boat roared up the lake. "Dad, aren't you going to chase it?"

"No, that's up to the police. We're so close to the lumberyard boathouse, I'm going to pull in and let you call Chief Mahoney."

As soon as the *Tall Timber* docked, Bert hurried off to Mr. Bobbsey's office.

He returned in a few minutes, panting. "The police launch is coming past here, and we're to follow it to the north end of Blueberry Island," Bert told the others. "The police are going to dock there and cut across to the cabin on foot."

"Why don't the police just dock at the Whitesides'?" Freddie asked.

"Chief Mahoney probably doesn't want to

alert them," Mr. Bobbsey explained, pulling the *Tall Timber* out onto the lake. "They might try to get away in their own boat."

As he spoke, a police launch with Chief Mahoney and several officers sped into view. Mr. Bobbsey guided his craft across the lake to join them.

A short time later, the *Tall Timber* swung behind the police launch, and both boats tied up at the dock on the north side of the island. The children climbed out to show Chief Mahoney the way to the Whiteside cabin.

Three of the police officers went ahead with the chief, while the fourth officer stayed with the driver of the police launch.

"Keep back," the chief ordered the children, "until we see if anyone's in the cabin."

Bert and Charlie followed the officers along the wooded path as Mr. Bobbsey trailed behind with the other children. When they reached the cabin, the officers broke down the door and went inside. Since no one seemed to be there, the officers motioned the older boys to enter.

Freddie, meanwhile, ran to peer through a wide crack in the boathouse wall. "Their boat's gone!"

"They've escaped," Mr. Bobbsey said, frowning.

"Maybe they're hiding," Nan said. "Let's go inside."

Upon entering the cabin, they found the officers searching the main room.

"Well, well," said the chief, holding up various garments from a suitcase. "The shoplifter was seen wearing outfits like these."

While the officers went through the boxes, Bert noticed that the section of floor he was standing on was loose.

"There could be a secret cellar under here," he told Chief Mahoney.

As the chief and another officer lifted the floorboard, the children gasped.

In the small storage space underneath cowered a woman!

"Mrs. Whiteside!" the boys exclaimed.

"Alias Mrs. Whiteside," the chief corrected them. "This is Mrs. Minnie Jones. I've seen her face on Wanted posters. Where's your husband, Minnie?"

The woman glared.

"Examine the rest of the floor," Chief Mahoney ordered the other officers. "Then one of you search underneath the cabin. Pen may be hiding there."

As the chief kept his eyes on Minnie Jones, he said, "Penman Jones and his wife are wanted in many towns for robbery and shoplifting."

Nan noticed the woman eyeing the bracelet on her arm.

"We just discovered your cave—with the stolen things *and* our dog inside!" Nan said.

Just then Tommy rushed into the cabin. "I've been watching from the woods," he said, trying to catch his breath. "Just before you got here, the motorboat with the man in it went south along the shore!"

"Penman Jones! He's going to the cave for the loot!" Bert said. "Charlie and I will show you the path to it, Chief."

"Fine," Chief Mahoney replied. He gave Minnie Jones a steely glance. "Why didn't you go with Pen? Given the chance, you would have, I'm sure."

Minnie glowered in silence.

"There probably isn't enough room on the boat for you *and* the loot," the chief went on.

"Pen always comes back for me," Minnie snapped.

"Take Mrs. Jones to our boat and bring her to the cave," Chief Mahoney said to one of the officers. "Nan, will you show them where it is?"

Nan nodded. Mr. Bobbsey said she could go with him in the *Tall Timber*. "The police launch can follow us. Freddie and Flossie, you come with Nan and me," he said.

"Yes, Daddy," Freddie said.

As the others headed back through the woods to where the *Tall Timber* and the police launch were docked, the chief said to the older boys, "Can Penman get his motorboat through the cave inlet? Is the opening large enough?"

"Yes. We figured he never took his motorboat there because it makes such a racket," Bert replied.

"In other words," the chief continued, "if you kids had heard the motor, you'd have found the cave sooner."

"Exactly," Bert said, leading the way to the maze.

As Chief Mahoney and two other officers stepped past the bushes at the entrance, the chief chuckled. "I can just see Penman losing one of his toupees in the shrubbery!"

The chief was still laughing to himself when Bert and Charlie lifted the stump and revealed the crude stairway. "Well, this is something!" the chief exclaimed, hurrying below.

Bert and Charlie followed, and looked behind the steps for the loot.

"It's gone!" Bert shouted. "All the bags are gone!"

Without stopping, he and Charlie rushed forward with the police officers. They had seen the tip of a motorboat shoved into the bushes. A man was sneaking toward it, clinging to the shadowy cave wall.

"There he goes!" Bert cried.

Shouting and confusion followed as the officers gave chase, but Penman slipped away from them. He jumped into his boat, started the motor, and backed quickly out of sight.

Meanwhile, Mr. Bobbsey, Nan, and the younger twins had rushed back through the woods to the dock. Behind them was a police officer with his prisoner, Minnie Jones, firmly in tow.

Nan asked her if she had lost a diamond ring in the woods.

"Yes, my engagement ring. You probably think I stole it, but it really is mine! Where is the ring?" Minnie fumed.

"At the police station," Nan answered.

Freddie scowled at the woman. "You took Tommy's big pail of blueberries and ate them, didn't you?" he asked.

The prisoner nodded sullenly and looked away.

At the dock, Minnie was taken aboard the police launch while the Bobbseys headed for the *Tall Timber*.

It wasn't long before the two vessels started off for the cave. The Bobbseys' launch took the lead. It rounded the end of the island and

whipped south, kicking up a trail of waves and foam.

"Watch for the entrance to the cave," Mr. Bobbsey said.

"It's under the knoll—the highest place along the shore," Nan said. She concentrated on the jungle of vines and bushes growing wild along the banks.

"There's the knoll!" Flossie exclaimed.

"And there's the inlet to the cave!" Nan said, signaling to the police.

The police launch shot ahead, but before it reached the veil of shrubbery, a motorboat sped through.

"Stop!" Nan shrieked.

"That's Mr. Penman!" exclaimed Flossie.

"Get him!" cried Freddie, jumping up and down excitedly.

The motorboat snaked swiftly through the water, followed by the police launch. Then, like a bolt of lightning, the launch streaked in front of the boat. The boat swerved to escape but the launch bore down harder. It bumped the motorboat, forcing it toward the bank until the boat slammed against thick vines and stopped. Penman Jones was trapped!

The Bobbseys watched as the two officers arrested him. They led him from his boat to the police launch, where his wife broke into a tirade.

"Good work, detectives!" an officer shouted to the children. "We'll get the other officers and take Pen's boat. You'll be glad to know it looks as if the stolen goods are all here."

Nan asked her father to pull closer to the police launch. "I want to ask Mr. and Mrs. Jones a few questions, if I may," she said.

"After all this, you deserve some proper answers," Mr. Bobbsey said, smiling.

When the two boats were side by side, Minnie said to her husband, "Those snoops found out everything."

Penman Jones gave the Bobbseys an angry look.

"Why did you hide that sack of loot on our boat?" Nan asked.

Penman grumbled, "I was running away after a robbery and almost got caught, that's why. The boathouse at the lumberyard was open, and I figured it was a good place for me to hide the stuff. Then those two"—he sneered at Freddie and Flossie—"came along and I hid the stuff in a hurry on the boat. Later, when the coast was clear, I went to the old wharf, where I had hidden my motorboat, and left."

"Did you wreck our maze and put a cord across the entrance?" Nan went on.

"Yes, we did," he confessed.

At that moment Minnie erupted. "We wanted you to quit what you were doing and leave the island. But no, you had to stick around and ruin all our plans."

Nan ignored the woman's outburst. "Who knocked down part of the maze when our dog chased one of you inside?"

"I did," Pen admitted. "The animal gave me a hard time until my wife came and helped me catch him."

"Good old Snap!" said Nan.

"Minnie Jones didn't lose the five hundred dollars Snap found, did she?" Freddie asked.

"No, she didn't," Pen replied sulkily.

Suddenly Flossie caught sight of Mrs. Bobbsey on the distant shore. "There's Mommy!" she said.

"And Sam and Bert and Charlie and the policemen!" said Freddie. The group was standing at the edge of the wooded path that led to the campsite.

Mr. Bobbsey guided the *Tall Timber* toward shore. After everyone swapped stories, Chief Mahoney said, "Speaking for the police and the people of Lakeport, I want to thank you all. You caught two very clever thieves and recovered much of what was stolen from Lakeport citizens."

The campers smiled. "We're glad we could help. It was fun," Nan said.

"There's only one person we still have to find," Bert said. "Aunt Emma."

"With a little luck you'll do that, too," the chief said.

The children waved good-bye as the police launch headed back to Lakeport. In a little while, the campers were back at the campsite. The twins took turns retelling about the capture.

Then Tommy came out of the supplies tent with Sam and Snap.

"Sounds like we're due for a celebration tonight," Sam said. "I'll build a bonfire."

Snap barked excitedly.

"Tommy, would you like to spend the night in our camp?" Mrs. Bobbsey asked. "We have an extra tent and sleeping bag."

"Neat!" Tommy said. "I'll go ask Mom." He raced across the clearing and later returned beaming. "I can stay!"

"Yippee!" the other children exclaimed.

The bonfire party that evening was a great success.

The next day when everyone bid Tommy good-bye, Charlie said, "Tommy, don't forget you're coming to stay with me in the fall when the school fair is on."

"You bet! I wouldn't miss it!" said the boy.

Standing on the beach, Tommy smiled wistfully as the *Tall Timber* swung back across the water away from Blueberry Island.

Later the Bobbseys pulled into the lumberyard boathouse.

"Well, I made my trial labyrinth and we solved a mystery," Bert said as he stepped off the launch. "I guess all our excitement is over for a while."

He didn't know that the twins would soon be involved in another exciting adventure in the *Mystery on the Deep Blue Sea.*

When the family reached home, Dinah greeted them at the front door. "Am I glad to see you!" she said as the twins gave her a hug. "There's a letter waiting for you!"

Bert ran to the hall table. On it lay an envelope addressed to the Bobbsey twins. He let out a whoop as he opened it.

"It looks like there really is an Aunt Emma," he told the other children. "Listen to this!"

Eagerly Nan and Freddie and Flossie clustered around their brother as he began to read the letter aloud:

"Dear Bobbsey twins,

"I am so happy and relieved that you found my five hundred dollars. Actually, it is only four hundred and ninety dollars since I spent ten of it.

"I met my niece at the railroad station on June 24th. After she handed me the money in a stack with a purple band around it, a woman poked her head out from behind the station. I knew she heard us talking. She saw the money, too.

"I knew about all the thefts in Lakeport so I decided to be extra careful with my money. I went across the street to a store and bought a game that came with play money. I put the real money in with it, except for the ten dollars that I stuck in my pocket.

"I was carrying a lot of bundles when I took a walk by the lake. A shaggy white dog ran up to me. I must have dropped my package when I was playing with him. The dog probably picked up the bag and ran off with it.

Mrs. Emma Ballard"

"Snap, you naughty dog," Flossie said.

"Here's something else," Bert said, reading on

"P.S. If you want to check my story, call

my niece's bank, the First National, in Westover. Her name is Sarah Ballard."

Since it was too late to phone the bank that day, Mr. Bobbsey called the next morning. A teller had seen the twins' ad in the newspaper and given it to Mrs. Ballard's niece. She had shown it to her aunt.

"Let's phone Chief Mahoney right away so he can send the money to Aunt Emma," Nan said.

Once more Mr. Bobbsey went to the phone. After the call, he said, "The police will contact Mrs. Ballard immediately."

"Fantastic!" Bert said. "Just wait till I tell Charlie."

As Bert leapt to the telephone, he heard a scratching sound on the back door and he went to open it. Snap trotted in carrying something in his mouth.

"Uh-oh, not another mystery!" said Flossie.

Freddie ran over to the dog. "Look, Snap found my missing flashlight!" he exclaimed.

"Snap sure has a knack for finding things," Nan said, "including mysteries!"